For Mom, Dad, David, and Michael – L.H.

For Mum, Dad, Emily, and Chris – S.K.

tiger tales

an imprint of ME Media, LLC
202 Old Ridgefield Road, Wilton, CT 06897
Published in the United States 2009
Text copyright © 2009 Laura Heiman
Illustrations copyright © 2009 Sophie Keen
CIP data is available
Hardcover ISBN-13: 978-1-58925-086-4
Hardcover ISBN-10: 1-58925-086-9
Paperback ISBN-13: 978-1-58925-419-0
Paperback ISBN-10: 1-58925-419-8
Printed in China

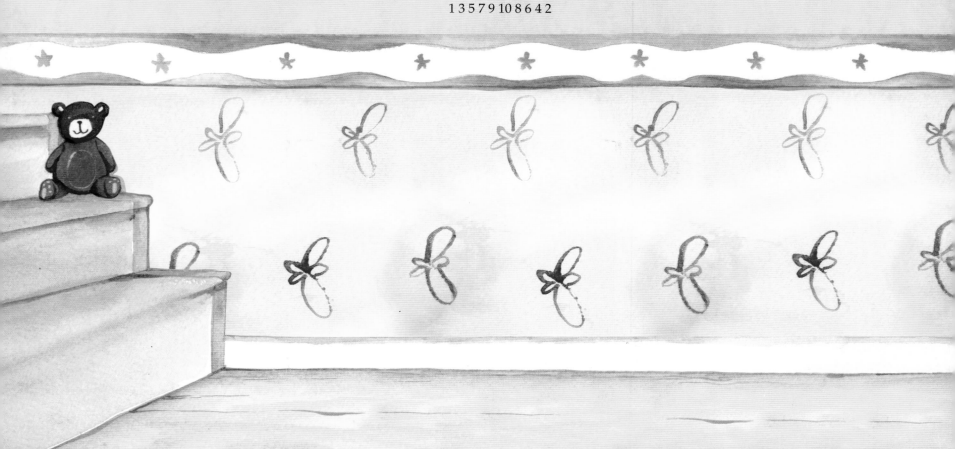

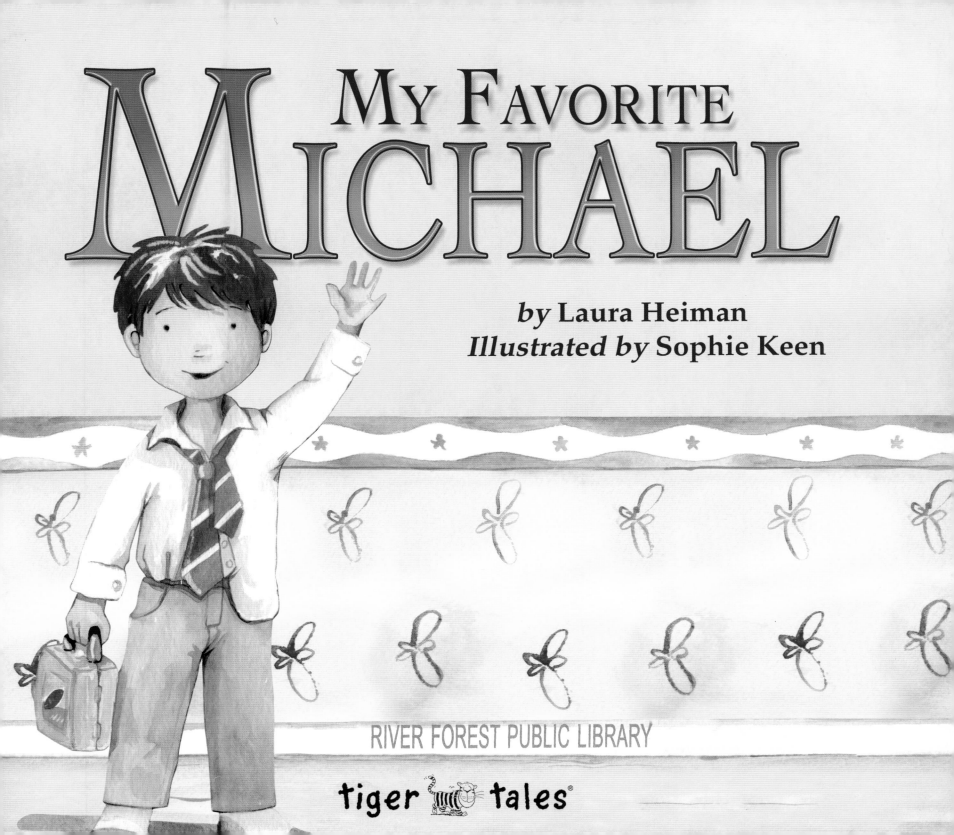

MY FAVORITE MICHAEL

by Laura Heiman
Illustrated by Sophie Keen

tiger tales

One morning, Michael woke up with a plan.
"I don't want to be just me today," he said.
"I'm going to be someone different."
Michael looked in his closet. He got dressed all by himself.

When he was done, he looked like his daddy.
"I'm Michael the businessman," he said. "I'm going to work."

In his office, Michael the businessman had a big day.

He wrote
important letters.

He put
paper in piles.

And he held a meeting.

But after all that sitting,
he wanted a vacation.

Michael went back to his closet . . .

and returned as someone else!

"I'm Michael the knight!" he said. "I'm off to save a princess trapped in the castle of a grumpy, old dragon!"

Michael the knight tiptoed toward the roaring beast.
Being a brave knight, he knew just what to do. He sang
a dragon lullaby.

Soon the dragon's snores could be heard across the kingdom.
"Shh," Michael the knight whispered to the princess. Together
they escaped and had many adventures.

They fought in a battle.

They danced at a ball.

And they traveled
to faraway lands.

But the princess grew tired.
The queen ordered her to
take a nap.

So Michael went back to his closet . . .

and came out with an "ARRGH!"

"Give me treasure or walk the plank!" growled Michael the pirate.
"You aren't a very polite pirate," said the ship's captain.
"Arrgh . . . please?"

Hearing the magic word, the captain opened the
treasure chest and handed over its booty.

"Yum!" said Michael the pirate. "I love treasure, especially the chocolate chip kind."

Michael the pirate
sailed the seven seas.

He buried treasure.

And he dug it up again.

But after many
voyages, Michael the pirate
sailed back home.

"Hmm," Michael thought. "I have been Michael the businessman, Michael the knight, and Michael the pirate. Who could I be now?"

Then he knew just what to do. Michael opened his closet one last time.

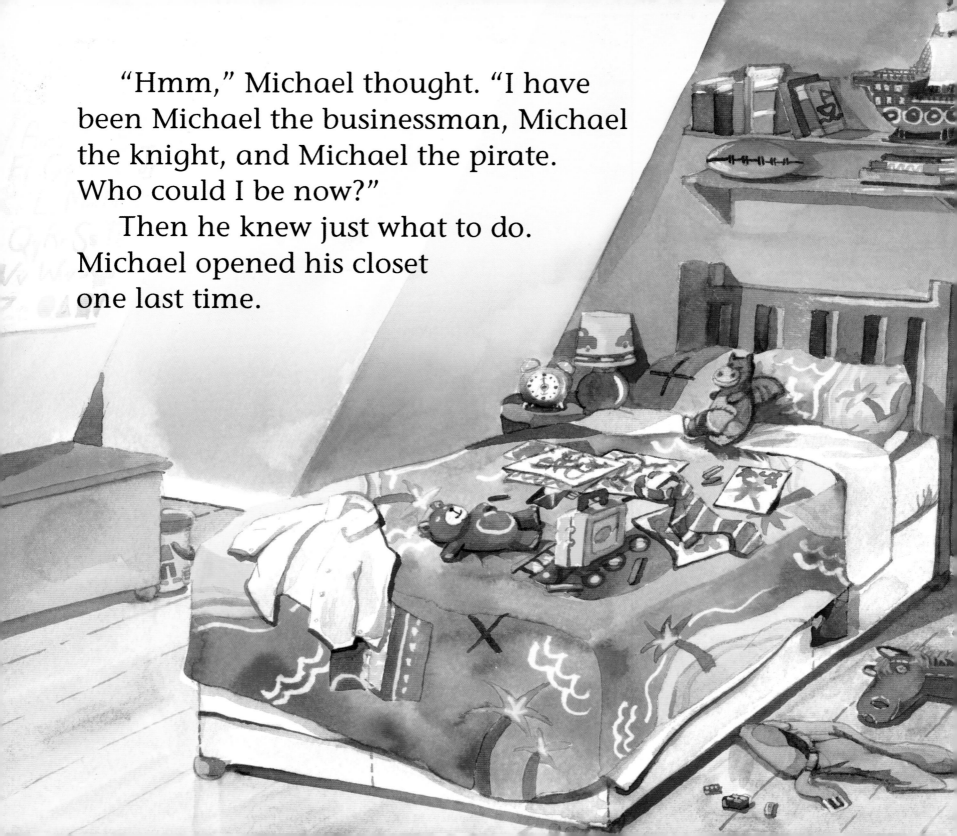

"Ta-da!" he said.

"Who are you?" asked his mommy. "Are you Michael the businessman?"

"No," said Michael.

"Michael the knight?"

"Nope."

"Are you Michael the pirate?" his mommy said.
"Not anymore," said Michael.
"So who are you?"

"I'm just Michael!"

"Oh, good," said his mommy. "I'm so glad it's you. Don't tell the others, but you're my favorite Michael."

"I know," said Michael. "I'm my favorite Michael, too!"